No part of this publication
stored in a retrieval system
form or by any means, wi

A CIP catalogue record for this book is available
from the British Library.

ISBN: 978-1-8382503-0-0
Published in the United Kingdom

The SugarCane boy, a publication of   TriAtis
Hillcrest House
26 Leigh Road
Eastleigh SO50 9DT

THE
SUGARCANE
BOY.

FOREWORD

Dear parents, thank you for buying this book which I hope is going to inspire your children. My name is Samuel T. Reddy, married and dad of three beautiful daughters. I am an author, speaker and advisor specialising in leadership development for career enhancement. As a multi award winning member of the British Armed Forces, I am based in Southampton, United Kingdom. But I was not always in the UK. The story you are about to read is partly my story as a boy growing up in Mauritius and partly fictional. I really hope it helps develop character in your children, build confidence and develop their creativity. The idea of writing this book came to my daughters who used to listen to my childhood stories before bedtime. Who better to tell them to your children now than my first born Alyssia.

SamuelTReddy.com

CONTENTS

CHAPTER 01

THE BEGINNING

Deep in the midst of the Indian Ocean, was an alluring island with the name of Mauritius and on this island was a boy named Sam whose heart was bigger than his head. He had ebony black hair and dark brown eyes and was always spotted wearing his signature sea-blue polo shirt and white shorts. On this island, there was also a little dog called Toby and coincidently, Sam and Toby were best friends who grew up together and had been through thick and thin- Toby was his pet but he felt so much more than a pet to Sam, it was almost as though their friendship was destined by fate! Some of Toby's characteristics and traits were that he was a little white dog who was very very playful and he and Sam would cause a large amount of mischief. They were inseparable, so much so that Toby would follow Sam on his journey to school.

Firstly, they would trek over a huge mountain which was called Mount Ory; it was fairly hard to climb as it was covered with a multitude of rocks that they had to jump over. However, all of their efforts were rewarding as when they reached its summit, they were welcomed with an absolutely scintillating view.

The turquoise of the sea blended into the pigmented blue of the sky creating the perfect ombre illusion. It was picturesque. From above, the oceanic breeze drifted upwards filling their noses with the heavenly scent of the salty ocean; the seagulls were cooing while the sea crashed into shore creating a mighty bang. The island that surrounded them was almost something out of a dream as the various pigments contrasted creating a kaleidoscope of colours.

Green leaves cascaded from the trees that were in the jungle, and they knew it as though it was the back of their hand. Inside of the iridescent, deep-blue ocean were numerous amounts of myths and mysteries that were begging to be solved. Up on top of the mountain, they would always rest and soak up the marvellous view and few peaceful moments, before racing one another down the mountain whilst simultaneously doing many forms of parkour. If upset, Sam would vent out his emotions by yelling at the top

"AAARRRGGGHHH!!!"

At the midpoint of the mountain was a large gap that had smooth ground where Sam and Toby liked to slide down on banana tree leaves! It was similar to sledding but as the weather in Mauritius was so hot, they never had the chance to experience snow, so mountain sledding was the closest thing that they could get!

At the foot of the mountain rested a sugar cane field which stretched as far as the bare eye could see; the shortcut that Sam and Toby grew to love was cutting through the field.

Large sugar cane towered over them which made it all

the more difficult to navigate, however Toby had a great sense of smell so he was able to use this as a compass.

Regardless of the time, they would have a little play around in the field and Sam would snap the top off of a sugar cane and throw it around for Toby to play fetch.

"Here Toby, fetch! Good boy!"

CHAPTER 02

HARVEST SEASON

During harvest season, the field would be stripped of its sugar cane which would leave a beautiful view in its midst, but it wasn't as nice as the mountain view; the air was so pure as the mountains would cleanse it.

Numerous amounts of wild pineapple and guava trees grew throughout the sugar cane fields and Sam and Toby would stuff their bellies to the point that when they returned home, they were not capable of eating dinner!

Wild hares inhabited the field and Toby was not

immune to chasing them! He would bark **"arf arf! Woof woof!"** as he chased them.

Once whilst they were playing, a hare caught Toby's eye and he began to chase it and forgot all about Sam!

"TOBY! Toby! Where have you gone? I'm lost without you!" Sam called out.

Since the sugar cane field was like a maze, it took him ages to find a way out but he eventually managed to escape the grasp of the maze. As he emerged, he saw Toby standing triumphantly over a hare before he let it go again.

"Oh Toby, you had fun then, didn't you? Please don't leave me in the field alone again."

He asked madly but he could not resist Toby's cute face and they began to play again. After playing in the field, they would continue their journey.

Toby would follow Sam on his way to school but he would stop at a specific bridge and they would part ways.

"Goodbye Toby! Remember, go straight home!
I love you and I'll miss you." Sam would say.

The bridge had a long, deep river flowing beneath it and their inquisitive minds would have loved to follow the course of the river to see where it would lead. However, time was against them as they spent far too much of it playing in the sugar cane field! They would spend countless hours in that field that Sam was often referred to as 'the sugar cane boy' by locals and relatives.

CHAPTER 03

BORING SCHOOL DAYS

During school, Sam would often daydream about the masses of adventures that they could have had: climbing the tall mountains until they reached the peak, swimming and diving into the cool ocean, exploring massive jungles and so much more! Most days his teacher would shout

"Samuel! Pay attention and stop daydreaming!"

Whilst Sam walked home, he became very lonely and would suddenly get a rush of excitement from thinking about going home to play with Toby!

As he was by himself, he would take a bit more time at the crossing of the bridge and stare down into the unknown for a while. All he could see was darkness, the bridge was so high that he was unable to see how deep the river was. In his opinion, this mysterious bridge should be deemed the highest bridge in the whole of Mauritius!

Since he walked home in the evenings, he would always see the sun setting and it was so mesmerising. On the other side of the bridge, the river's path led to the ocean and in the distance, the sun would be setting on the horizon; Sam loved to watch the sunset as he found it relaxing, therapeutic and majestic.

He loved to wonder and imagine where that river led to: the other side of the island or a cave that delved into the earth or even potentially another land!

He would frequently remind himself of his promise that one day, some day, he would explore the river and partake on one of the greatest adventures of his life with his faithful best friend alongside him. But he would always snap back into reality as he remembered Toby and would rush home.

Once he arrived home, he would open the door and Toby would leap on top of him and they would play for a while even though Sam was supposed to be doing his homework!

"Toby! I missed you, how was your day?"

and Toby would respond by licking Sam's face. Their relationship was as though they were siblings and they loved one another as brothers: Sam was an only child so they spent so much time together and they never got bored! As he walked through the house, he would be met with a delicious waft of spices from his mum's cooking.

Every day they would walk to school and follow their

usual routine of trekking up the mountain and playing in the field. Somehow, they never got tired of that routine as together they could do anything and make it seem fun! One time, the consequence of Sam being late for school was that he had to clean and rearrange the whole of his back garden, but Toby helped him and they managed to turn a chore into a game in no time!

However, on their journey to school one day, they witnessed a little dog being thrown into

'THE VAN'...

The van that would take dogs away and end their lives... the van that every pet owner dreaded to see. Every time they passed the van, they would hear dogs whimpering for help from within the walls, however they were unable to do anything so they sombrely passed by.

"One day we will free those poor dogs, I promise." Sam would whisper.

He had a longing to free the dogs, but the men who captured the dogs were big, muscular, contemptible and daunting. Sam was no match for them.

CHAPTER 04

LOST

One day, on their journey to school, they were enjoying themselves so much that they completely lost track of time.

As they passed through the sugar cane field, they saw a massive guava tree that stretched taller than ten times Sam's height.

On the top of the tree rested masses of big, juicy guavas; they were so mouth-watering that Sam felt the urge to climb it.

With Toby cheering him on, he began to climb the guava tree until he got to the top and managed to pick the biggest guava of all! When he got down, they opened up the guava and had such a feast, they slowly ate it up, savouring every delicious piece as though it was the rarest thing on earth. That is what made them oblivious to the time and inevitably made Sam late for school.... again.

Later that afternoon, on his way home from school, Sam prepared himself to face the wrath and anger of his parents and was stressed about it all the way home.   When he arrived home, he was met with a sombre look from his parents and they didn't utter a word about him being late for school. Something was wrong. Sam could feel it in his gut and it wasn't the type of feeling he wanted to be right about. An hour after he had gotten home, he realised that he hadn't seen Toby at all and went to ask his parents.

"Mum, Dad, where is Toby?"

"I can't seem to find him anywhere," he asked. But he was met with the vague response of

"He is probably playing outside or hiding somewhere..."

Sam called out for Toby several times but no Toby came running to him. He went to ask his parents again if they had seen his dog.

Eventually, they told him that Toby hadn't returned from when they had parted ways at the bridge this morning.

"Toby hasn't come back home yet... I'm sure he's fine." muttered his parents.

They tried to reassure him but worry overtook Sam and he went to search everywhere for his dog.

"Tobyyyyyy. Oh, Toby boy!
Where are you? "

"I miss you, come back to me!" he would chant everywhere he went. He walked all the way to school, through the sugar cane field, up the mountain, in the jungle and still nothing. Toby was nowhere to be found...

A week went by and …. still no Toby. Sam searched for his dog every single day but no success.

Filled with sadness, Sam walked to school for the rest of the week with a massive hole in his heart. Friday afternoon he arrived back home to see his parents sitting at the dinner table once again, their faces showing a variety of emotions as they told him that they had found Toby...

"**Sam, we found Toby...**" his dad told him.

All the sadness was replaced with immediate joy and he started jumping up and down- but something wasn't right, his parents still looked upset.

When Sam asked if he could go and play with Toby, his parents looked at each other and added,

"There's something we need to tell you; Toby is in the living room but he came back and we think...
we think that he had a fight with another dog."

Sam pushed past his parents and raced into the living room and there he saw his Toby. His left ear had been ripped off and was hanging on by mere threads; his normally pearl white fur was stained with crimson blood; his back was a map of cuts and bites. Sam fell to his knees and began to cry over Toby who was barely clinging to life.

"Toby. Oh Toby. Who did this to you...?" he uttered between sobs.

CHAPTER 05

CRIMSON WATERS

Later that night, they had to give Toby a bath in the attempt of getting rid of his bloodstains. As they lifted Toby into the basin of warm water, he began to whimper so they loosened their grip and gently placed him in. The warm water soothed his pain and he soon stopped whimpering as the water turned a crimson red from the blood that had been washed away from his wounds. He lay motionless in the water; he had fallen asleep. Carefully, they lifted him into his little bed and began to pat him dry. A few hours later, Toby woke up from his slumber and gently nudged Sam, who was still by his side.

Sam got up to his feet, gave Toby a sad look and went to get some food. From outside the dining room, he could hear his parents indistinctly talking.

"…. **injured… give away… Sam… Toby… pain…**"

As soon as he entered the room, his parents stopped talking and walked away… Sam could tell that something was wrong, was it Toby?

No, it couldn't be, he had already begun to heal, he will be fine, right? By the time Sam got back to Toby, he was peacefully asleep on his bed again. See, nothing to worry about.

Sam spent the night asleep next to his furry friend to make sure he was comfortable and rested.

The following Saturday morning, Sam's mum gave him 100 rupees and asked him to go and buy a bag of flour, even though they already had 3 full bags at home.

"Would you go and buy a bag of flour right now please Sam?"

His mum practically shoved him out of the door before he could protest! Sam was adamant that something

was wrong, so he ran as fast as his legs could carry him and this resulted in him almost knocking an old lady over!!

"Watch where you're going young man!"

she scolded while he replied **"Ma'am I am so sorry."** whilst continuing to run at the same time.

In the shop, he grabbed the first pack of flour that he set his eyes on and paid for it without having a polite discussion with the shopkeeper like he normally would have done.

"Good morning Sam! How are you today?" the shopkeeper asked. As Sam was in a hurry, he politely nodded and dashed out of the shop.

Then, he began to run home past the sugar cane

field, but it was a bit more difficult as the bag of flour weighed him down, so he snapped off a bit of a sugar cane and bit into it and was instantly refreshed with a boost of energy.

All of a sudden, he began to run faster than he ever had before, it was as though something had given him the power of superspeed...

As he got to his road, Sam saw something very strange. And then it all clicked... it was 'The Van!' The van that took sick dogs away...His heart grew heavy. He knew what was happening.

He dropped the bag of flour to the floor and it broke apart spilling everywhere like a white cloud.

Sam sprinted to the van, but it was too late. It had already sped off.

He looked at the van with tears in his eyes and longing in his heart. Then he turned to face his mum and dad. He had never felt so angry before.

"HOW COULD YOU DO THIS TO HIM, HE WAS GOING TO GET BETTER, HE

WAS GOING TO GET BETTER!"
Sam yelled.

"Sam..." his mum pleaded.

As he began to see red, he started screaming at his parents and then ran into the house straight to his room. Broken, he slowly sunk to the floor and started to cry as his heart shattered into a thousand different fragments and his anger turned into pain. Hands quaking, he tried to hold his head in the attempt of silencing his tears. Every memory of Toby resurfaced and each memory was like a dagger that pierced deeper and deeper into his heart. A million thoughts banging in his head, he began to drown in his own tears.

Sam refused to leave his room or eat breakfast for the rest of the weekend: he was drowning in his own misery. Eventually, Monday morning, he got out of bed and began to trudge to school without uttering a word to his parents.

Everything he saw reminded him of Toby. The mountain where they would race one another up and Toby would always win. The sugar cane field where they would frequently get lost and play fetch with one another. Everything he saw was a painful memory of his best friend, his brother, his Toby. As he dashed through the sugar cane field, he suddenly felt so angry that he snapped a sugar cane and bit it so hard that when he swallowed the juice, he was overcome with a shuddering sensation. With all of his self-control, Sam contained his anger and slowed down to walk to the bridge while energy pulsed through him.

CHAPTER 06

ADRENALINE

Toby and Sam had always longed to see where the river led to, but now without Toby, Sam's aspirations had crumbled into dust and they would never have the chance... This was the bridge that they would normally say goodbye, but Sam never got to say goodbye, Toby had been ripped from his grasp and taken in front of him while he stood transfixed, helpless, alone.

As Sam sadly crossed the bridge, he wiped tears from his eyes and something caught his eye... Was his vision deceiving him? He rubbed the tears away and saw that it was really there.

'The Van!'. He thought "Could Toby still be in the van…"

Then he realised what he had to do. Mustering all his strength, he ran towards the van but it started to move!

Strangely, Sam was catching up with the van and he had never run this fast before!

Just like before, he was overcome with this powerful sensation that allowed him to do the impossible and out of the ordinary... Whilst

he ran, his mind buzzed with the thought of what was allowing him to have this superspeed; the only thing he had done differently was eating the sugar cane.

Was that what was granting him these superpowers? With his speed matching the speed of the van, he chased it over a long distance without getting tired. When the van finally came to a halt, Sam decided that now was the time to make his move. Quietly, he crept towards the van and began to pick the lock. Time was slowly ticking away and he had to hurry up. In frustration, he hit the lock with yet another newfound force and it shattered, with a loud bang on the floor.

CLANGGG. ...

Panicked, he looked around but thankfully no one had heard it!

Sam gently guided all of the dogs out and there he saw him.

TOBY!

Toby jumped onto Sam and they embraced for a long time. It was as though time had momentarily stopped. However, Toby's wounds hadn't begun to heal. All of a sudden, the door slammed shut but luckily all the dogs had managed to get out. A big man towered over them and started to shout.

"OI! WHAT DO YOU THINK YOU'RE DOING!! STOP! STUPID CHILD! "

The only option left was to run! The dogs scattered in all directions. Sam picked Toby in his arms and they began to run towards the sugar cane fields in the effort of losing the man there. They got inside the field and began to run towards the mountain. After a few minutes, they stopped and looked behind them.

They had lost him!

CHAPTER 07

WHERE THE WATER FLOWS

They climbed up the mountain and there he was finally able to see how badly Toby was hurt. Sam was overcome with a great wave of sadness and he began to cry over Toby.

A single tear fell from his eye and landed on Toby's ear as a ray of sunlight from above shone down on them. It began to shine and glow, with a gentle bang, it had gone and Toby's wounds were no more! After this, he remembered his theory from before: that somehow the sugar cane gave him a special ability...

He looked up at Sam and said **"thank you,"** and Sam replied **"you're welcome"** before realising that Toby had spoken to him!

Confused, he realised that he could hear Toby in his head despite him not actually talking.

He could hear Toby thinking **"I understand that this is a strange experience for you, but it will all make sense."**
What a strange day this had been...

His tears healed Toby, he has super strength, super speed and could talk to Toby!

It was almost as though the sugar cane had granted him some sort of power; he didn't understand it but he made the decision not to tell anyone before he properly understood what was happening.

For the duration of the day, they played in the sugar cane field like never before. Sam decided to experiment and would bite a sugar cane to see how fast he could run and the difference was commendable!

The sugar cane also allowed him to shake a coconut tree hard enough so that the coconuts would fall down!

They were having so much fun that Sam had completely forgotten that he had school and he also forgot about his parents as well. By sunset, they were sat at the top of the mountain; Toby was by Sam's side as they looked at the beautiful orange, yellow and red of the sun blend into the now navy sea; Sam could not have been happier.

"I love you Sam,"

Toby whispered lovingly and Sam replied **"I love you so much too."**

Suddenly, he realised that his parents must be worried to death and the moment was gone.

They jumped to their feet and raced one another home. Before walking inside his house, Sam took a deep breath, let out a sigh and walked in.

His parents were sat at the dinner table, their heads in their hands with worry etched onto their faces. As Sam walked in, they sharply looked up and strode towards him embracing him with a big bear hug. Sheepishly, Sam looked behind him as Toby trotted in and his parents let out an evident gasp. Reluctantly, he explained the story to his parents and after much discussion, they eventually agreed that they were allowed to keep Toby as he was healed and no longer in pain.

"This is incredible! A true miracle!"

his mum proclaimed.

The next day, they were playing fetch whilst walking to school.

They were having so much fun that Sam accidentally threw the sugar cane into the river. Curiosity overtook them and they decided to venture down the river. Carefully they went to the side of the bridge and climbed over the railings where they began their rocky descent.

There were parts of the river that they had to go through as the land was too rocky to tread on; luckily both Sam and Toby knew how to swim because the current was very strong!

"Be careful Toby! The current is strong!!"

he warned. Sam took off his school shoes otherwise they would get ruined. As the current of the river was so strong and fast, the sugar cane stick was no longer in their sight! If Sam was being honest, the sugar cane was just an excuse to go on an adventure down the river. The river had many twists and turns and Sam guessed that the river probably led to the sea. Nevertheless, they still wanted to find out where it led to...

After climbing over various rocks and having to cross the river, they saw that it led to a cave that they had never seen before. Strangely, the cave had lights shining from the inside.

ABOUT THE AUTHOR

At 14 years old Alyssia is one the youngest author in the UK & in Mauritius. She is the winner of the young writers award 2020 in the UK, a school librarian and class captain. Alyssia has been passionate about books from the age of 7. She is a 1st generation of British-Mauritian born in Southampton England and speaks English, French & Creole.

www.TheSugarCaneBoy.com

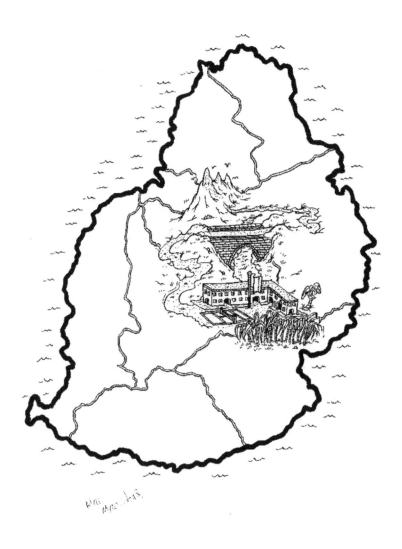

Printed in Poland
by Amazon Fulfillment
Poland Sp. z o.o., Wrocław

63421554R00031